WORM
D · A · Y

BY HARRIET ZIEFERT
ILLUSTRATED BY
RICHARD BROWN

MR ROSE

A BANTAM SKYLARK BOOK®
TORONTO · NEW YORK · LONDON · SYDNEY · AUCKLAND

Sally

Mr. Rose's Class

Jennifer

Richard

Adam

Emily

Mr. Rose

Matt

Jamie

Kelly

Justin

Sarah

RL 1, 006–009

*This edition contains the complete text
of the original hardcover edition.*
NOT ONE WORD HAS BEEN OMITTED.

WORM DAY

*A Bantam Book / published by arrangement with
Little, Brown & Company Inc.*

PRINTING HISTORY
Little, Brown edition published June 1987

*Skylark Books is a registered trademark of Bantam Books,
a division of Bantam Doubleday Dell Publishing Group, Inc.
Registered in U.S. Patent and Trademark Office and elsewhere.*

Bantam Skylark edition / September 1988

*Bantam Books are published by Bantam Books, a division of Bantam Doubleday
Dell Publishing Group, Inc. Its trademark, consisting of the words "Bantam
Books" and the portrayal of a rooster, is Registered in U.S. Patent and Trademark
Office and in other countries. Marca Registrada. Bantam Books, 666 Fifth Avenue,
New York, New York 10103.*

I remember children from my classes in
South Orange, New Jersey and Rye, New York:
Jonathan, John, Peter, Priscilla, Penny,
Ellen, Tex, Beanie, Mark, Barbara, Marc,
Terry, Darlene, Eric, Ricky, Cathy, Julie,
Michael, Margaretta, Susan, Gail, David,
Johnny, Judy, Debbie, Louis, Jeffrey,
Karen, Liz, Gary, Cheryl, Steven, Amy, Muriel,
Andy, Robert, Diane, Abby, Dawn, Joanne,
Larry, Jane, James…

CHAPTER ONE
RED WIGGLERS

"Good morning, class! It's Tuesday,"
   said Mr. Rose.

"Good morning, Mr. Rose."

"Are you ready to hear the plans for today?"
   Mr. Rose asked.

"We were ready yesterday," said Richard,
    "but you wouldn't tell us."

"You wouldn't want me to ruin the surprise,
    would you?" said Mr. Rose.

"Are we having a picnic?" Sarah asked, eyeing
    the white Styrofoam cooler in front of
    Mr. Rose.

"No, Sarah. No picnic today!"
    Mr. Rose answered. "There's not
    a single peanut-butter-and-jelly
    sandwich in here—not even one."

"Awwww," the class groaned.

"Then what *is* in there?" Sally asked.

"Two hundred live animals!" Mr. Rose declared
    with a smile.

"Oooh! Can I see?" Kelly pleaded.

Justin shouted, "Those animals must be pretty small!"

"They *are* small," Mr. Rose said. "And they don't have fur, or ears, or even legs."

Sarah, who thought she knew everything, said, "I know what you have."

"Tell us," Mr. Rose answered.

"You have a bunch of worms!"

"Sarah," said Mr. Rose, "this time you are absolutely right!"

"Worms are yucky!" Matt said.

"I don't like worms either," Jennifer added. "They're disgusting."

"Calm down, everybody," said Mr. Rose. "Let me explain what we're going to do."

Mr. Rose lifted the cover of the cooler.

He shoved his hand inside.

He picked up a handful of peat moss and said,
   "You can call this *worm dirt*."

He walked around and let everybody have
 a good look at the dirt.

"It's moving!" Sarah said.

"Right!" Mr. Rose answered. "It's moving
      because it's alive with red wigglers."

"Eww!" said Jennifer, squirming in her chair.

"I bet I know why they're called red wigglers,"
      said Sally. "They're red and they wiggle!"

"How'd you guess?" said Mr. Rose with a smile.

Mr. Rose walked to the front of the classroom.
He said, "I'll give each of you a scoopful of
dirt on a paper plate."

"Do we *have* to touch the worms?" Jennifer asked.
Mr. Rose said, "Don't be scared. Worms are
harmless. They don't bite. They don't
sting. And they don't talk back."

"You mean like we do!" Richard yelled.

"Right! But anyone who doesn't want to touch
worms can handle them with a plastic spoon,"
Mr. Rose continued. "Now, who wants to
help me give out the worms?"

"I do!" Jamie said.

"I do, too," Adam said.

Adam always wanted to do what Jamie did.

"Clear your tables, everyone," said Mr. Rose.
"Jamie and Adam will give each of you
a plateful of worms."

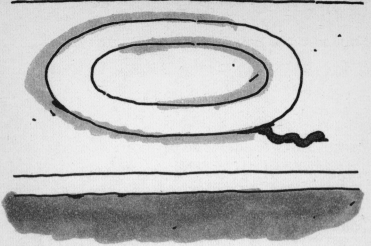

"This worm likes to crawl under the plate,"
    said Jamie. "It doesn't like it out in the open.'
"Why do you think that is?" asked Mr. Rose.
"Maybe it's scared," answered Jamie.
"Maybe it's your bad breath!" said Richard.
  Jamie stuck her tongue out at him.
"What are some other possible reasons?"
    Mr. Rose asked.
"It could be cold," said Kelly.
"Or, it might not like the light,"
    said Sarah.
"Good," said Mr. Rose. "Keep thinking
    and watching and you might find out
    which is right."

"Look at these two worms," Jamie said.
"They're tied up in knots!"

"Let me see!" yelled Adam.

"Me, too!" yelled Richard.

"Worms stuck together like that are usually
mating," Mr. Rose said.

"How?"

"The eggs from one worm are being fertilized
by the sperm from the other."

"My mother told me all eggs need to be
fertilized before they hatch," said Jamie.
"Right?"

"Right," Mr. Rose answered

Adam got a magnifying glass.

"Is this an egg?" he asked. "It's brownish white."

Adam let Jamie take a quick look
at the small circle inside the worm.
Then he grabbed another worm.
He watched it move for a long time.
He was trying to figure out if the front
of the worm squished together first when
it moved, or if the back did.

Jamie wanted the magnifying glass.

"Give it to me," she said.

"But I'm using it," Adam answered.
"I hardly ever get to use stuff,
and whenever I do, you want it."

"Uh-uh!" Jamie said. "You're the one
who always copies what I do!"

"What's going on?" Mr. Rose asked.

"Adam won't share the magnifying glass,"
Jamie answered.

"I think I know where to find another one,"
Mr. Rose said. "I'll get it. In the meantime,
please share."

When Mr. Rose walked by, Matt asked,
  "Can I measure a worm?"
"What do you think?" Mr. Rose asked.
"I think I can," said Matt. "I think
  I can do it with a ruler."
"But the worm scrunches up and stretches
  out!" Emily cried.
"Will you measure the worm when it's long
  or when it's short?" Mr. Rose asked.
"I guess I'll measure it both ways," Matt said.
"Good idea!" said Mr. Rose. "Maybe you can
  find out just how much a worm can stretch."
"That sounds hard!" Matt answered.
  Matt wasn't so sure he could do things
  by himself.
"Come on, give it a try," said Mr. Rose.
"Can I help?" Richard asked.
"Sure!" said Matt.
  Richard was good at math and Matt was
  happy to have his help.

"Attention everybody!" called Mr. Rose.
"I'm putting some questions on
the board."
Mr. Rose found some chalk and wrote:
What happens...

when one worm meets another worm?

when a worm bumps into a pencil?

when a worm comes to the edge of a desk?

What happens?
Mr. Rose's class will try to find out.

CHAPTER TWO
WORM EXPERIMENTS

Mr. Rose put all kinds of things
on the science table.
There were plastic boxes and jars.
There was plastic tubing, black paper,
tinfoil, tape, and paper cups.
Justin counted four pails, three shovels,
two ant farms—without ants—
and one big washtub.
Good stuff!
All of it good stuff for experiments.

"Do worms like hot or do they like cold?"
    Emily asked.
"I don't know if they like hot or cold,"
    Matt said. "But I know they like puddles."
"How do you know?"
"When it rains, the worms come out and
    crawl into puddles," Matt answered.
"They all die in the puddles," Emily said.
"They do not. Sometimes there are fifty
    worms in a puddle, and they're gone
    the next day," Matt insisted.
  Mr. Rose heard the conversation.
"Maybe you can make a puddle in this
    washtub," said Mr. Rose. "Then you can
    watch and see if the worms head for
    the puddle, or stay in the dirt."
"I think there's something in the water
    that worms like," Matt said.
"I think worms are dumb. They head for
    puddles, then they drown," Emily said.
"I think you need to find out who's right,"
    Mr. Rose said.

25

Suddenly there was a commotion
near Jamie's table.

"Quiet over there!" yelled Mr. Rose.
"What's happening?"

"Adam is on the floor!" said Jennifer.
Mr. Rose ran over. "Adam, are you all right?"

"I'm fine, Mr. Rose," Adam said.
"I'm worm-walking."

"Worm-walking!" cried Jennifer.
"What's that?"

"It sounds like something we should all
try outside," said Mr. Rose. "Right
now, everyone back to work."

Adam stopped wiggling.
He said he would help Emily and Jamie
find out if the worms liked wet or dry soil.
Jamie put wet dirt and dry dirt
on different sides of a box.
She dumped a handful of worms on the dry side.
She announced, "I think the worms are going
    to crawl over to the wet side."
"How do you know?" Adam asked.
"I think Matt's right. Worms like water,"
    Jamie answered.
"I don't think you can be sure until you
    experiment," Adam said.
Adam felt smart—smarter than Jamie.

DRY
DIRT

WET
DIRT

Emily said, "I'm going to use sand.
I'll sprinkle half with water and put
my worms on the wet side."
Adam looked at Jamie and Emily and said,
"Since you're starting your worms on
either the dry or the wet side, I'll
start mine in the middle."
"Good idea," said Mr. Rose. "But I have
two questions for you."
"What are they?" Adam asked.
"Is your dry soil as dry as Jamie's?
Is your wet soil as wet as Emily's?"
The questions made Adam stop and think.
And he realized maybe he wasn't as smart as
he thought he was—at least about worms.

Emily, who was sometimes nosy, looked
toward Kelly's table.
Kelly and Jennifer had an ant farm.
They were watching what the worms
were doing underground.
"They're so lucky," Emily said.
"They don't have any better stuff than
we have," Adam said.

"How do you know?" Emily asked.

"I know we should stick to what we're
doing and not try to copy them,"
Jamie said.

"Who's copying?"

"Not me," Adam said.

"Not me, either," said Jamie.

"Attention, again," called Mr. Rose.
"I'm still hearing questions, so I'll add
them to the list."

Do worms live under rocks?

Do worms eat dirt?

Do worms chew?

Do worms make tunnels?

"Now we'll go hunting for the answers
to these questions," Mr. Rose said.

"Hunting?"

"Yes, we're going on a worm hunt. I'll
bring pails and shovels. Line up."

CHAPTER THREE
GOING ON A WORM HUNT

Mr. Rose took the lead.

The class followed him to the vacant lot
next to the school.

Mr. Rose looked at his watch and said,

"I'll give you five minutes to find worms."

Mr. Rose continued, "Just to make it a
    little more fun, no tools allowed.
    At least not for now."
Everybody ran in different directions.

Soon Mr. Rose said, "Your five minutes
are up. Come back."

"I found my worm under a rock," Sarah said.

"Mine was under some leaves," Justin said.

"I looked under leaves," said Emily, "but I
didn't find a worm. I found a slug!"

"Yuck!" said Jennifer. "They're so slimy!"

"Oh, you don't like *anything*!" said Matt.

"My worm is long and skinny," Richard said.
  "I found it when I dug up some dirt."
"No fair!" Matt said.
"Sure it's fair," Mr. Rose said. "I said no
    tools, but I didn't say you couldn't
    dig with your hands."

"We dug together," said Emily and Jamie.
   "And here's our worm!"
"Wow!" Sally said. "That's the biggest worm
   I've ever seen. It must be six inches!"
"Don't be silly!" Sarah said. "It's big,
   but it's not six inches."
Sarah always tried to show how much she knew.

"Did everyone find a worm?" Mr. Rose asked.

"I didn't," Adam said.

"Neither did I," Matt said.

"You said you didn't like worms," Sarah said. "Maybe that's why you didn't find one."

"Guess so," Matt said.

"Put the worms in this pail," Mr. Rose said.

"Now, who can guess how many worms I'll
find in a shovelful of dirt?"

Mr. Rose dug into the ground.
Then he held up a shovelful of dirt and
asked for guesses.

Sarah said, "Five."

Richard guessed three.

Justin said, "Eight."

"Who wants to find out how many worms
are really here?" Mr. Rose asked,
pointing to the shovel.

"I will," said Emily.
She liked getting dirty.
Emily sifted through the dirt.
She found one worm, then one more,
and that was all.

"Richard's guess came the closest," Mr. Rose said.
"What will happen if you dig deeper?"
    Kelly asked.
"I think he'll find more worms," Sally said.
"It's not good enough to say 'I think,'"
    Mr. Rose said. "Let's try it."
Mr. Rose dug deeper.
Emily checked the soil and found one worm.
So what Sally thought wasn't true.
At least it wasn't true for where Mr. Rose
put his shovel.
Maybe if Mr. Rose had dug in another spot,
Sally would have been right.
Maybe.

Emily had a good idea.

She said, "Let's pour water here and
see if the worms come up."

"But they won't come up right away," Matt
said. "They're slow crawlers."

"So we'll wait," Richard said. "Then we'll
check this spot."

Sally called from the other side of the lot.
"Come here, everybody! Look what I found!"
Everyone ran to see what Sally found.
It was a salamander.
"It's so cute!" Sarah shouted.
"It is cute," said Mr. Rose. "But after
everyone has seen it, please put it
back. It will be hard to keep a
salamander alive in the classroom."

There was a big rock in the lot.
Jamie and Emily decided to roll it
on its side.
They wanted to see what was underneath.
Adam felt left out. He said,
   "I bet you can't push that
      big rock. You're too weak!"
Jamie and Emily pushed and pushed.
The rock didn't move.
"I told you it wouldn't move," Adam said.
Jamie and Emily pushed harder
and harder and harder.
The rock moved—
right onto Adam's toe!
"OUCH! OUCH!"

Adam screamed loud enough for Mr. Rose
and all the others to hear him.
"Now what's wrong?"
Adam was crying and couldn't talk.
"This time he *is* hurt," said Jennifer.
Emily said, "It was an accident!
We were trying to push the rock
and we pushed it onto Adam's
foot by mistake."
"He was in the way," Jamie said.
"They did it on purpose!" Adam cried.
"I'm sure Emily and Jamie didn't mean
to hurt you. You were probably
standing too close. Let's see your foot,"
said Mr. Rose, taking off Adam's shoe.
Mr. Rose slowly bent Adam's toes—
one at a time. It hurt, but only a little.
Mr. Rose didn't think Adam had any
broken toes.
Adam said, "I feel better."
Jamie said, "I'm sorry."

"I think you'd better go to the nurse's office,
    Adam," said Mr. Rose.
"Do I have to?" Adam asked.
"It would be a good idea to have it
    checked. Can you walk?"
"I can hop," Adam said with a smile.
"We'll help him," said Emily and Jamie.
  So Jamie, Emily, and Adam walked—
  and hopped—back to school.
  They even tried some worm-walking
  along the way.

CHAPTER FOUR
WIGGLE WIGGLE

Back in the classroom, Mr. Rose gave everyone
time to check their experiments.
Jamie went to look at the handful of worms
she had dumped in the dry dirt.

"Look at my worms," Jamie said. "They're all
    still there, except two."
Emily, who put her worms in wet dirt, said,
    "One of my worms crawled to the dry side.
    The rest are still where I put them."
Just then Adam came back
from the nurse's office.
"What are we doing?" he asked.
"Checking our worms," Jamie said.
"I'll check mine too," Adam said.
Adam found out his worms had all moved
to the wet soil.
Jamie did some adding in her head.
She said, "There are more worms in wet dirt
    than in dry dirt. So worms like wet
    better than dry. What I said before was right."

"Wait a minute," Mr. Rose said. "What about all those worms still in the dry soil?"

"They'll move," Jamie answered. "They're just slow."

"What if they don't?"

"I'm still right," Jamie said.

"You're stubborn," Emily said. "Just like my brother."

"How could you make Jamie change her mind?" Mr. Rose asked.

"By experimenting again," Adam said.

"Scientists repeat their experiments many times until they're sure," Mr. Rose said.

"Do we *have* to do this again?" Jamie asked.

"I think it would be a good idea," Mr. Rose said. "Why don't you put your box on the table by the window? Then you can check it later."

"Attention," called Mr. Rose. "I've been talking to Adam, Emily, and Jamie. They're still not positive worms like wet better than dry dirt, so they're going to repeat their experiments."

"How many times is enough?" Justin asked. "Ten?"

"That sounds like a good number," Mr. Rose said. "At least for now."

"Should we clean up?" Sarah asked.

"I was just getting ready to tell you to clean the tables and put away the equipment."

"What about the worms?"

"Put them all back in the cooler," Mr. Rose said. "And I'll give them a snack."

"What do worms eat?" asked Richard.

"Water and cornmeal," answered Mr. Rose. "Doesn't that sound good?"

"NO!" yelled the class.

Mr. Rose chuckled. "Well, then I guess we'll just have to have juice and cookies!"

"Hooray!"

"As soon as the room is clean!" added Mr. Rose.

Everyone wanted to eat, so clean-up
went quickly.

The snack helpers gave out the food.

The classroom was pretty quiet.

Everyone was busy eating.

Suddenly there was a screech.

"EEK!"

"What's wrong?" Mr. Rose asked.

"THERE'S A WORM UNDER MY PLATE!"
Jennifer shouted.

"So, pick it up," Adam yelled.

"Give it to me," Mr. Rose said. "I'll put it
with the others."

Jennifer did not want to pick up the worm.
She was upset.
She was sure someone put it there
on purpose.
"What's wrong, Jennifer?" Mr. Rose asked.
  Jennifer cried, "Richard left the worm there
    to tease me."
"Did you?" Mr. Rose asked Richard.
Richard nodded.
Mr. Rose had a private talk with Richard.
Then Richard picked up the worm and
put it back in the cooler.
Wiggle. Wiggle.

Mr. Rose turned to the blackboard again.
"We've asked ourselves a lot of questions
about worms today. Can anyone give me
some answers about worms?"
"Worms can sense what's around them,"
said Kelly.
"Worms like to hide under things," said Jennifer.
"Worms like water!" said Jamie.
Adam said, "We still don't know that for sure."
"But you always see them in puddles," said Matt.
"And they live close to the top of the
ground, where rain can get to them,"
added Emily.
"And Mr. Rose said they like water
as a snack!" said Richard.
Mr. Rose was pleased. "You've done
some good thinking today, class.
It looks as though Jamie's idea
might be right."
Jamie smiled proudly.

"*But*," Mr. Rose continued, "before
we can say for sure, we'll have
to do more experiments."
Adam felt better.
Jennifer raised her hand.
"Yes, Jennifer?" asked Mr. Rose.
"I learned something else about worms
today," she said.
"And what's that?" Mr. Rose asked.
"They're not really *that* icky, but I still
don't like them under my plate!"
Everybody laughed.

The bell rang.

It was time for everybody to go home.

What are we going to do tomorrow?"
   Sarah asked.

I have something planned," Mr. Rose said,
  "but I want to keep my plans a secret."

Please tell," Kelly begged.

You can wait," Mr. Rose answered. "You can
   wait until tomorrow. Class dismissed.
   See you Wednesday!"

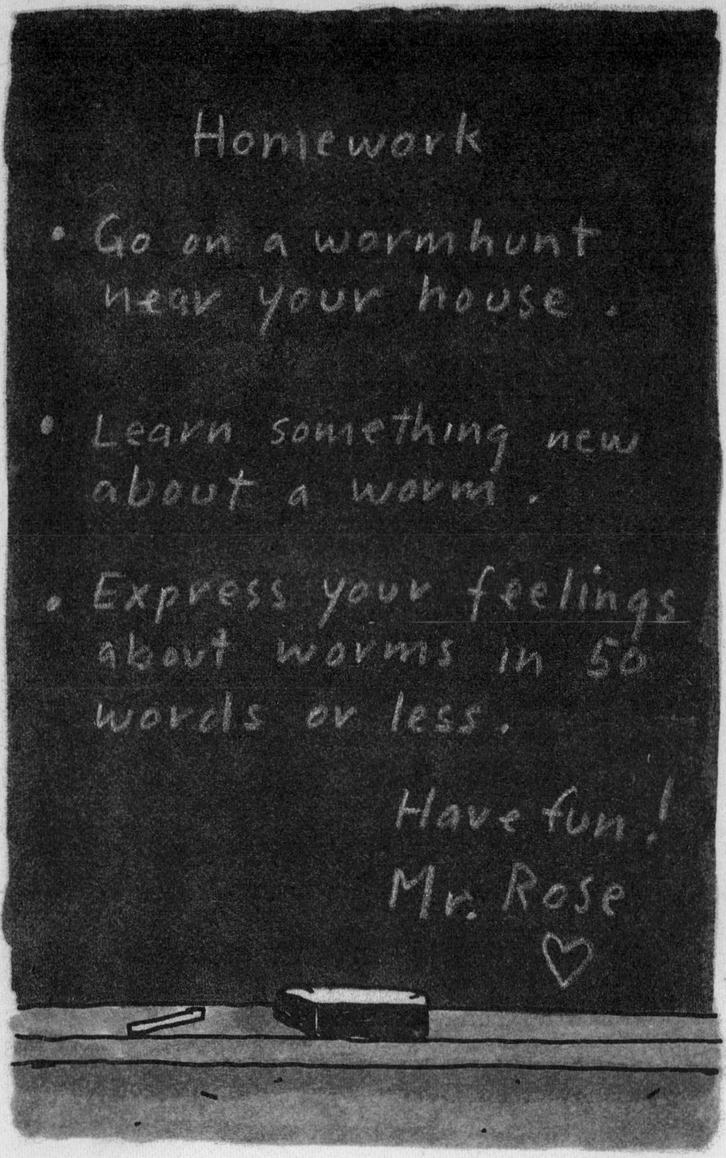
Homework
• Go on a wormhunt near your house.
• Learn something new about a worm.
• Express your feelings about worms in 50 words or less.
Have fun!
Mr. Rose